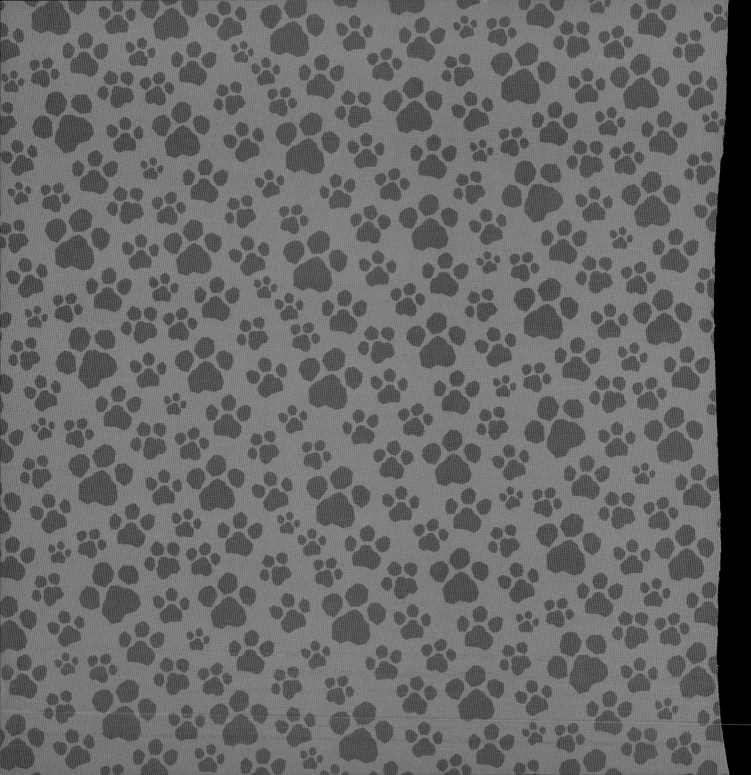

This storybook belongs to

....

DEAN

First published in Great Britain 2022 by Dean, a part of Farshore
An imprint of HarperCollins*Publishers*
1 London Bridge Street, London SE1 9GF
www.farshore.co.uk

HarperCollins*Publishers*
1st Floor, Watermarque Building, Ringsend Road
Dublin 4, Ireland

©2022 Spin Master Ltd. PAW PATROL and all related titles, logos, characters;
and SPIN MASTER logo are trademarks of Spin Master Ltd.
Used under license. Nickelodeon and all related titles
and logos are trademarks of Viacom International Inc.

ISBN 978 0 0085 5858 1
Printed in China
001

A CIP catalogue record for this title is available from the British Library.

Stay safe online. Farshore is not responsible for content hosted by third parties.

MIX
Paper from
responsible sources
FSC™ C007454
FSC
www.fsc.org

This book is produced from independently certified FSC™ paper
to ensure responsible forest management

For more information visit: www.harpercollins.co.uk/green

Pups Save Ryder's Robot

Zing!

Ryder is switching on **his new robot, Robo-dog,** for the first time.

"OK, Robo-dog ... sit!" says Ryder.

"That's such a cool robot," says Skye.

"Thanks, I've just finished him," says Ryder. "Let's try digging!"

Ryder presses a button and **Robo-dog tunnels underground** at top speed.

Ryder peers down the hole. "Where did it go?" he says.

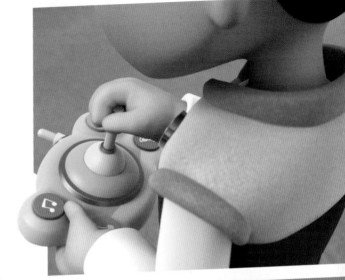

Zuma is asleep in his Pup House when Robo-dog pops up right underneath him.

"Whoa! Where did you come from?" says Zuma.

Ryder races around the corner. "Sorry, Zuma," he says. "I see you've met Robo-dog. Let's try ... flying instead!"

Robo-dog's paws turn into rockets and he floats up into the air.

"Wow!" everyone says.

"It should be able to run really fast, too," says Ryder.

Ready...
Set...

"No robot can
outrun me!" says
Marshall. **"Let's race."**

Chase gets the pups
into position, then
uses his megaphone
to shout, "GO!"

GO!

I'm okay!

Marshall and Robo-dog start to race, but just as Marshall takes the lead, he trips and rolls into a log.

"I'm stuck!" shouts Marshall.

"Hold on," says Ryder, pressing the robot's **'Turbo Power'** button.

Robo-dog goes even faster, pushing Marshall out of the log with a *POP* and zooming ahead.

Marshall tries to keep up, but stumbles into Ryder, who sits on Robo-dog!

Oof!

"Oh no! **The antenna is broken**," says Marshall.

Robo-dog jumps up, twitching and buzzing. Ryder tries to stop it, but the robot digs a tunnel and disappears!

Suddenly, Robo-dog appears on Main Street.

It flies straight into Mr Porter's fruit stall and then he knocks Mayor Goodway off her feet.

Mayor Goodway calls Ryder. "**Ryder, help!** Someone's pet is on the loose!"

"That's my robot," says Ryder. "It's out of control, but we'll take care of it!"

"PAW Patrol to the Lookout!" says Ryder.

The pups line up in the Tower, ready for action.

"**We have to stop Robo-dog** before it causes any more problems," says Ryder. "If we can turn it off, I can try and fix it."

"Skye, with your zoom goggles, you should be able to spot it. And Rocky, I need you to help us build something so we can catch it."

"Let's take to the sky!" says Skye.

"Green means go!" barks Rocky.

"The rest of you, please tidy up the mess Robo-dog has made," says Ryder. **"Let's roll!"**

Pups away!

Skye is in the helicopter looking for Robo-dog.

"He's heading towards the water tower," says Skye.

Robo-dog crashes into the water tower and out of the other side. Then it flies straight through the pet shop.

Katie and Cali jump out of the way ... and into the bath.

"Guess he didn't want to use the doggie door," says Katie.

Smash!

Rubble and Zuma are on Main Street tidying up.

"Here's the last of the watermelons, Mr Porter," says Rubble.

"Thanks for helping, pups!" says Mr Porter. "I think we got all of it."

But suddenly, Robo-dog appears and knocks them all over again.

Rubble sighs.

Skye calls Ryder on her helmet mike.

"Ryder! Your robot is heading straight for me!"

"Can you get him to fly towards Rocky's truck?" Ryder says.

"I'll do my best!" says Skye, looping away from the runaway robot.

Meanwhile, Rocky has made something to catch Robo-dog — a **magnet launcher**.

"Almost ready!" says Rocky.

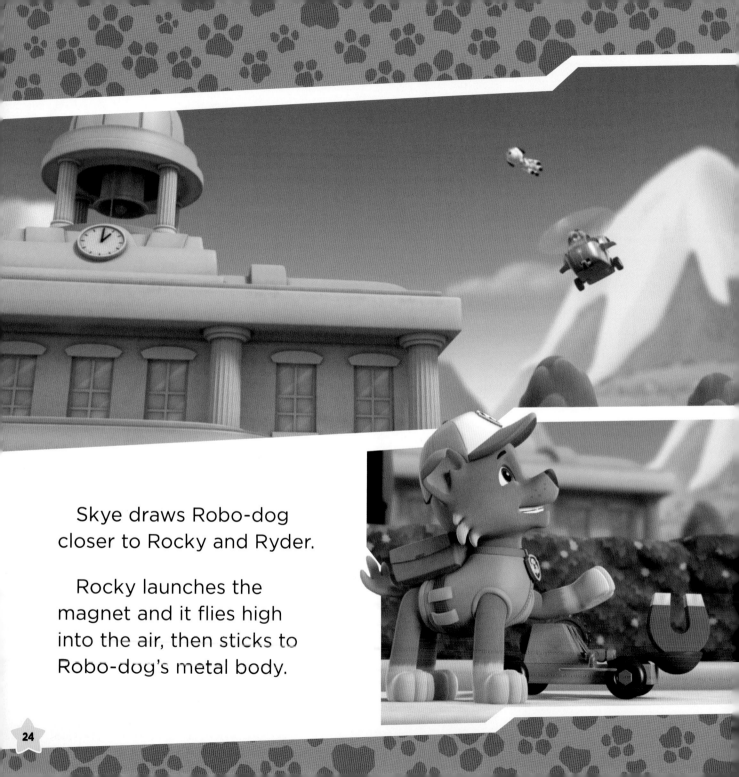

Skye draws Robo-dog closer to Rocky and Ryder.

Rocky launches the magnet and it flies high into the air, then sticks to Robo-dog's metal body.

Whizz!

"**Perfect shot, Rocky!**" says Ryder. "You're on, Skye."

Skye lowers the helicopter's hook and catches the magnet. "**Robo-dog is coming home!**" she barks.

Skye lowers Robo-dog onto Mr Porter's patio.
It tries to run around but **Ryder turns it off**.

"I guess it's back to the drawing board," says
Ryder, sadly.

"Hold on, Ryder," says Rocky. "I've got an old antenna you can use."

Ryder changes the antenna and switches on Robo-dog.

The robot is back to normal. **_BARK! BARK!_**

"Thanks, Rocky! And thanks to all you pups, too," says Ryder. "I couldn't have fixed it without you!"

"Well, if you're ever in trouble, Ryder ..." says Rocky.

"Just yelp for help!" all the pups bark.

"What a bunch of good pups," says Ryder, smiling.

THE
END

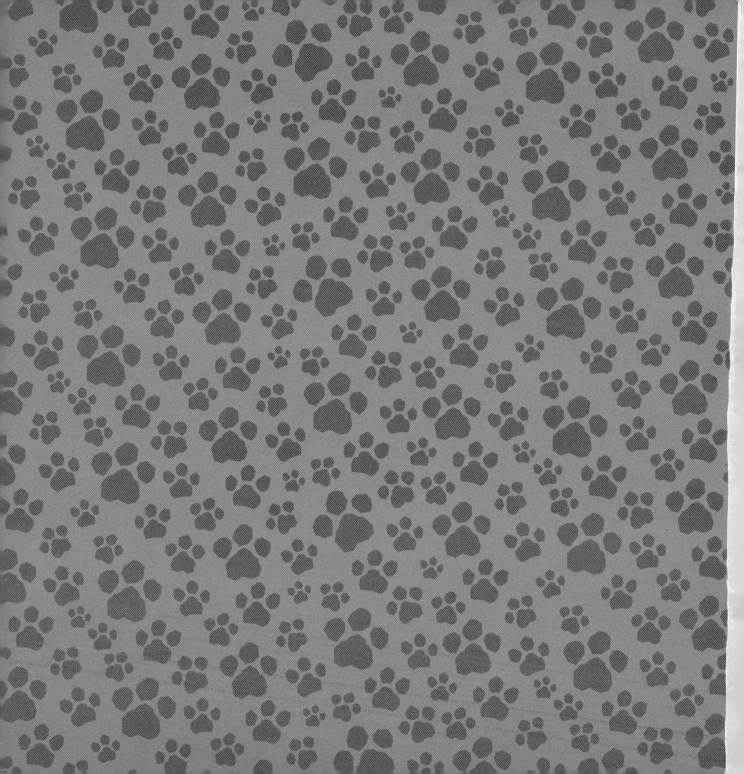